Published by The Dial Press
1 Dag Hammarskjold Plaza
New York, New York 10017

Manufactured in Great Britain/First U.S.A. Printing

Library of Congress Cataloging in Publication Data
Oram, Hiawyn. Skittlewonder and the wizard.
Summary: A retelling of how Prince Skittlewonder
breaks the spell put on him by an old wizard.

1. Fairy Tales.   2. Folklore-Scotland

I. Rodwell, Jenny. II. Title.
PZ8. 063Sk 398.2'1'09411 [E]   80-11646

ISBN 0 8037 7833 3   ISBN 0 8037 7834 1 (lib. bdg.)

SKITTLEWONDER
AND

THE WIZARD

HIAWYN ORAM/JENNY RODWELL

The Dial Press/New York

Once upon a time there was a young prince. From the time he woke up till the time he went to bed, he played skittles. He had become so good at the game, everyone called him Skittlewonder.

One day a strange old man appeared at the castle and offered to play the prince in a contest. "But if you lose," he warned, "you'll fall under my spell forever."

"I never lose," said the young prince, which was true at the time. They played their hardest, but as luck would have it, the old man won.

"Find out my name and where I live by Christmas or you'll turn into a set of skittles yourself," and so saying, the old man disappeared.

Not wanting to waste any time, for there were only seventeen days left till Christmas, Skittle-wonder quickly packed a few belongings, kissed his mother good-bye, and strode off through the palace gardens in search of the strange old man.

"I knew no good would come of being skittle-mad," sobbed the Queen.

The prince walked for four days and four nights. On the fifth day he came upon a gypsy knitting butterflies that flew off almost before she had finished them.

"Unravel that one," she said, nodding in the direction of a large blue and purple specimen, "if you know what's good for you."

Skittlewonder followed and unraveled the butterfly until on its last stitches it fluttered into the windy turret of a castle.

There the prince found a witch playing ball with a cat. She looked so pretty that he poured out his story at once.

"It'll be that wicked old Wizard Green Sleeves," she said. "He lives on the river Ugg, eight hundred miles from here. Take one of my magic bouncing balls and a pair of my winged slippers and you'll be there by sunset."

Skittlewonder winged and bounced his way through the skies, until he came to the river and a gigantic castle carved out of a mountain.

He went up and knocked loudly on the door. Almost immediately the old man who had beaten him at skittles appeared. Seeing the prince, he tried to shut the gates, but Skittlewonder put his foot firmly under the door and shouted, "Your name is Wizard Green Sleeves and this is where you live."

The Wizard howled with disappointment at being found out. "You don't get off that lightly," he snapped. "There are still three Impossible Tasks for you to perform before you are free of my spell. I'll give you a bed for the night and in the morning we'll see just who is who!"

He took Skittlewonder into his dining room where seven beautiful girls sat eating their supper.

"These are my daughters," said Green Sleeves. "They will give you food and show you where to sleep."

That night the prince lay in a great gold bed, wondering how anyone could perform the impossible, when he heard the door creak and saw a beautiful girl creeping toward him.

"I'm Lily, the Wizard's youngest daughter," she whispered, laying a golden box on the bed. "Before you begin any of the Impossible Tasks, knock once on the lid, whistle twice into the wind, and open this box."

Next morning at breakfast the Wizard was in high spirits.

"Your first task, Skittlewonder," he sneered, "is to build me a palace from a stone from every quarry in the world, covered in feathers of every kind of bird in the world. And all in one day."

The prince said good-bye and, hiding the magic box under his coat, went into the countryside.

Once out of sight he carefully drew out the box, knocked once on the lid, whistled twice into the wind, and opened it. To his astonishment out flew thousands upon thousands of birds.

"What is your will?" they asked.

The prince told them of the first Impossible Task and with a great rushing sound the birds flew off into the sky. In a few hours they returned, each with a stone in its beak. They plucked a feather, each from another's tail, and set to work.

Before the prince's eyes and by sunset, a castle of stone and feather sprung up, glowing as if it were made of precious jewels.

The Wizard was furious. That evening at supper he stabbed and jabbed at his toad pie.

"Tomorrow, young upstart, your Impossible Task is to sow a barrel of corn seed, grow it, harvest it, and replace the corn in the barrel all in one day."

Then he settled down to supper, content, for he was sure no one could make a field of corn grow in a day.

At dawn the next morning the prince hid the magic box under his hat and set off into the countryside. Once out of sight he took down the box, knocked once, whistled twice into the wind, and opened the lid. This time out flew millions of fairies.

"What is your will?" they asked.

The prince showed them the barrel of seed and told them of the second Impossible Task.

As he watched, the fairies emptied the barrel and sowed the seed. The moment it touched the earth it grew six feet high and by midday was ripe and golden. Then taking their knives from their belts, the fairies reaped the harvest, threshed it, blew the chaff into the wind, and returned the corn to the barrel.

The impossible was done and it was only teatime.

Green Sleeves was so angry at the prince's success that he refused to come in to supper at night. But Skittle-wonder and the Wizard's daughters could hear him pacing up and down in his room and muttering angrily to himself.

Next morning the Wizard was looking tired and grumpy. He complained that the food was not cooked enough and threw his toast around the room.

"Today," he yelled, "your Impossible Task is to find my grandmother's golden needle that was dropped fifty years ago in the Forest of Density and Darkness, and all by lunchtime."

Then he sat back to drink his tea, playing the edge of the table as if it were a piano, for he knew that the forest was so dense and so dark, you couldn't see your hand in front of you.

This time Skittlewonder slipped the magic box into his lunch basket and set off into the countryside. At the edge of the forest he took it out, knocked once, whistled twice into the wind, and opened the lid. Out flew mile upon mile of elves.

"What is your will?" they asked.

The prince told them of the third Impossible Task, and the elves, who can see in the dark by their candles that never go out, flew into the forest. In no time at all they were back with the needle.

Skittlewonder returned to the Wizard's castle, and holding up the needle, he bowed politely to the Wizard.

"Your grandmother's golden needle, sir. Now am I free of your spell?"

"Th–th–that's n–n–not the right n–n–needle!" he stammered, and grabbing at it, he pricked his finger. As a drop of blood fell there was a whirring sound and the Wizard was suddenly a small mouse.

"Grandmother's curse, curse Grandmother's curse!" squeaked the mouse, scuttling away beneath the floorboards.

Lily and her sisters jumped up and hugged the prince. "You've freed us from our wicked stepfather!" they cried.

That evening there was rejoicing far and wide. Everyone from the river Ugg country came up to the castle and danced and sang and ate up all the ex-Wizard's supply of food.

The prince opened the magic box and let the birds and the fairies and the elves out forever.

Then he asked Lily if she would marry him.

Lily agreed and first thing next day they winged and bounced their way · back home in time for Christmas.

The Queen was over-joyed. Looking at Lily, she said to the King, "At least something's come of the boy being skittle-mad!"

Then they all sat down happily to Christmas dinner.